LILY WOOL

LILY WOOL

Paula Vásquez

GIBBS SMITH
TO ENRICH AND INSPIRE HUMANKIND

Lily Wool is a white and black sheep. Even though she looks like all the others, she has a mind of her own.

The herd doesn't understand her; they say
she is from another planet.

While the other sheep are
sleeping and dreaming of
juicy beets...

Lily is awake counting stars and dreaming of other things.

During the day, Lily skips through the meadow
instead of grazing on the tasty grass.

She tries to behave like the other sheep, but Lily gets bored of so much grazing and resting.

For Lily, a thread of wool
sparks her imagination.

She uses it to become the
best gymnast of the herd . . .

the fastest rider of the meadow . . .

or to catch the biggest fish of the ocean.

helps a friend,

plays Cupid . . .

or becomes a writer.

once upon a time

But then . . .

she hears the herd calling her name.
"Lily Wool!"

"What have you done?"

The sheep do not look happy.

Lily quickly puts her imagination and creativity to work making use of the loose wool,

and finds a way to help others.

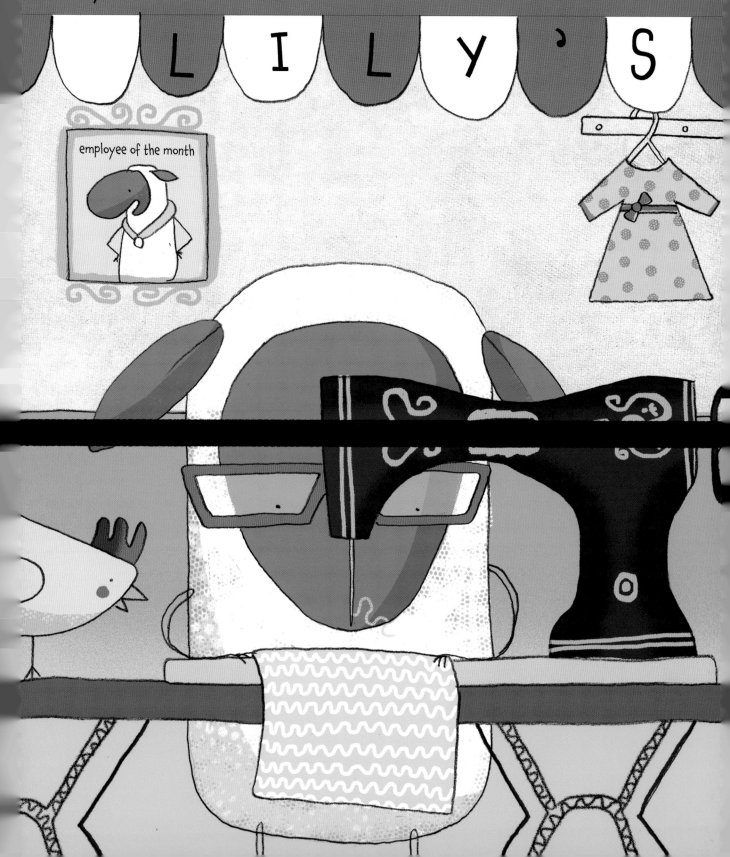

She has discovered her special place in the herd.

Now they understand how fun
imagination can be.

Paula Vásquez, an avowed artist from childhood,
studied graphic design at the Universidad Católica
de Chile, and honed her illustration skills with a post-
graduate diploma from Finis Terrae University. She
continued her studies at EINA Escola de Disseny i Art
in Barcelona, Spain. She currently lives in Santiago de
Chile writing and illustrating children's picture books.

Manufactured in Hong Kong in July 2017 by Paramount Printing, Co.

First Edition
21 20 19 18 17   5 4 3 2 1

Published by
Gibbs Smith
P.O. Box 667
Layton, Utah 84041

1.800.835.4993 orders
www.gibbs-smith.com

Editorial consultation by Janice Gibbs Horschel
Designed by Paula Vásquez
Gibbs Smith books are printed on paper produced from sustainable PEFC-certified forest/
controlled wood source. Learn more at www.pefc.org.

Library of Congress Control Number: 2016959883
ISBN: 978-1-4236-4728-7